Cheated

(The story of a father who would not give up his children)
A DOCUMENTED ACCOUNT OF PARENTAL ALIENATION SYNDROME (PAS)

by

Ronald E. Smith and Ariel D. Smith

PublishAmerica
Baltimore

© 2007 by Ronald E. Smith and Ariel D. Smith.
All rights reserved. No part of this book may be reproduced, stored in a retrieval system or transmitted in any form or by any means without the prior written permission of the publishers, except by a reviewer who may quote brief passages in a review to be printed in a newspaper, magazine or journal.

First printing

All characters appearing in this work are fictitious. Any resemblance to real persons, living or dead, is purely coincidental.

ISBN: 1-4241-7306-X
PUBLISHED BY PUBLISHAMERICA, LLLP
www.publishamerica.com
Baltimore

Printed in the United States of America

DEDICATION

This book is dedicated to my first born, Richmond Elihu Smith, who was born on May 9, 1986. Richmond is currently fighting for his life with liver cancer and I want him to know that under no uncertain terms it was he who transformed my life on that day in May when he opened his eyes and looked into mine for the very first time. I want you to know that this event will be forever burned into my memory, for eternity. It was you, son, who gave me the right to use the word parent for the first time in reference to myself and it was you for whom my love has grown exponentially day by day since the very first day we met. You have always tried to beat me at chess, go-cart racing or arm wrestling and, although in those instances you always fell just a little bit short, what you did was win the most important part of my being and that is my heart. I pray to the Almighty that your body heals and you live a long and productive life. Moreover, because we have been cheated out of your formative years, I pray that God gives us an opportunity to know one another as men.

God Bless You, Son!!!
Love, Dad

Prologue

One of the most alarming statistics found about divorces is the amount of children who are having little to no contact with the non-custodial parent. Twenty-one million Americans have died as a direct result of the increased divorced rate, including one million divorce-related suicides and one million divorce related homicides in the twentieth century alone.

Unless there are extenuating circumstances, parents deserve the opportunity to share equal responsibility in raising their children, meaning, in the context of financial and daily life duties. However, as we have found, even with court orders, a custodial parent can refuse to allow the children to interact with the non-custodial parent, and do this with little or no backlash. If the custodial parent goes unpunished for their noncompliance of court orders then they are able to carry on their regime of complete control over their children's daily lives.

Non-custodial parents who cannot continue to afford to hire a lawyer to help fight for a fair judgment relating to custody, is left almost completely vulnerable to the decisions that the custodial parent chooses to make. The law does little to limit the custodial parents' ability to make on-the-spot resolutions to custody agreements.

Indeed, there are laws and penalties in place for parents who do not pay child support or do not adhere to the court orders pertaining to custody, but there is no enforcement mechanism in place for non-compliant custodial parents. When the custodial parent has the majority of the control over the children, the job of keeping the non-custodial parent out of their lives is made that much easier. This happens to many people throughout our society and I happen to be one of the parents subjected to this crime. I am now a licensed and ordained minister who is committed to assist all non-custodial parents in their quest to have shared, quality time with their children.

The battle I fought over custody of my children, and the extent I went to maintain the time I was given, with my children, forced me to form an organization dedicated to seeing that every parent is given a fair opportunity to be a part of the lives of their children. The relationship I fought to have with my children is the driving force behind all of my efforts.

Non-custodial parenthood has become this nation's fastest growing poverty stricken subculture with negatively contributing factors from parental alienation syndrome, paternity fraud, a corrupt, illogical, child support collection system and the Friend of the Court whose questionable practices and declaration of abandonment of divorced parents further adds to the dilemma that we are already facing. These are some of the reasons that I formed Children Need Both Parents, Inc. in 1993. What I do for non-custodial parents today I was not able to accomplish for myself in the past. A portion of the proceeds of this book will be donated to Children Need Both Parents, Inc. so that we may continue the fight for shared parenting. I believe that strong families make strong neighborhoods, which make strong cities, which make a strong nation. We as a nation are only as strong as our families. We must begin to realize that what is in the best interest of our children is a balanced diet of mother and father working together in an unselfish effort to raise strong productive members of society. Our family court system must reinvent itself and become an ally and a contributing faction of this realization. I would like to offer special recognition to four men who have become highly recognized foot soldiers in the quest to change laws and take away the stigma given to non custodial parents and they are Jim Semerad (Dads and Moms of Michigan); Dan Diebolt (Fathers Rights Council); Robert Pederson and Darrick Scott-Farnsworth (A Child's Right). These four men have worked tirelessly in the quest for shared parenting in the state of Michigan. If in fact, the laws are changed in the state of Michigan and ultimately throughout this entire nation, it will be in no small part because of these men.

All characters appearing in this work are fictitious. Any resemblance to real persons, living or dead, is purely coincidental.

Proud Papa

It's Saturday, June 10, 2006, and Roger Scott is standing in the auditorium of Francis W. Parker High School, in Chicago. The high school graduation and commencement ceremony has begun for the class of 2006. His son, Aaron Scott, who is now eighteen, is the reason that he is present for this ceremony. He is standing at the base of the stage, with camera in hand, anxiously waiting for the perfect moment to snap a shot of his son accepting his diploma.

While standing there he begins to feel an overwhelming sense of grandeur and reconciliation. He begins to light up inside because at this moment, he realizes that his ex-wife is no longer in control of his relationship with his children. She can no longer hinder the ability to foster a solid, father-son relationship with his sons.

Today became a milestone (or graduation of sorts for him, as well). Aaron, the younger of his two sons, not only graduated, but has also turned eighteen and now is considered an adult. Roger has completed the duties as a non-custodial parent and is no longer legally attached to their mother. He can now reconcile himself with the pain of the last twenty years. He no longer has to pay his ex-wife child support, nor does he have to subject himself to court appearances, mediation or court orders in order to spend time with his children.

His ex-wife spent most, if not all, of the children's lives trying to keep him from them. Roger's two sons meant everything in this world to him and she knew it, but that didn't matter to her. With the assistance of the judicial system, he suffered mental and emotional abuse at the hands of his former spouse.

It was the love for his children and his naivete, which made him vulnerable to that exploitation. However, he now feels that he can now move on. That time in his life is history and was one of the worst mistakes ever made, or one of the greatest life lessons ever learned.

Delia is his ex-wife and the mother of their two sons, Richard and Aaron. They met in the summer of 1983 at a theater audition for the play, *Cat Fish Row Chicago Style* (a rendition of *Porgy and Bess*) put on by XBAG (the Experimental Black Actors Guild).The auditions for the play were held within Parkway Community House, a community center located on the south side of Chicago. This was one of Roger's very first activities in Chicago after returning home after graduating from the University of Michigan-Dearborn.

He auditioned for the part of Porgy and won the role. Delia played as an extra and offered technical support to the director. It was during the production of that show that they came to know each other. At that time, he was twenty-three and she was thirty. In his mind, she was what younger men commonly refer to as a "vet" and the prospect of dating a thirty-year-old was extremely intriguing.

In the beginning, the relationship was strictly plutonic. They would chat on the set of the play, meet at a restaurant with the other actors, or occasionally, go to her house to listen to records and talk.

As time progressed, the relationship turned physical. The two never considered themselves dating, and he never considered her as nothing more than a friend. He loved the bachelor lifestyle and his freedom too much to give any woman true consideration. He was a young and naïve man and felt at that time women were nothing more than a conquest.

She dated other people, as well, and seemed to be okay with the inclusive relationship. They saw each other for about a year, but that eventually dwindled and faded.

By March of 1985, he had not spoken to Delia, in months. During that time, Roger moved from his mother's home where he had moved into following his return from college, into his own apartment. One-day Roger came home from work and found a note stuck in the mailbox and it read, *Why did you just disappear, please, give me a call...Delia.*

He was surprised, since they had not talked in months. He then realized that he never told her where he lived and oddly enough, he did not even question how she got the address. Instead, he responded to her message with a phone call.

When they talked, it was as if nothing had changed, not even time. She talked about the things that were taking place in her life and he did the same. Not long after this, he received a phone call from her telling him that she was pregnant by a man that she really did not want to have children for and was considering terminating the pregnancy. At that time, she did not want the father to be involved or even know that she was pregnant for that matter. Her dilemma was that she needed someone with her during the abortion because she was not sure whether she could drive back home after the procedure and she thought that Roger, being the person that he was, would do her this favor. He agreed to assist her by taking her to the clinic and driving her back home safely. She arrived at his apartment on a Saturday morning about 7:00 a.m., the two of them got into the car and she gave him the directions to the clinic. He took her there and waited until she was ready to go home. When she got into his car, she requested that she stay with him for the balance of the day and would return home on Sunday because she did not want to be alone after a procedure of this magnitude. Roger was truly disappointed in her because of the decision that she had made with her unborn child, but out of concern for her as a person, he stayed with her until she was mentally ready to go back home and deal with the life that she was leading.

Roger was involved in what his company called the "Presidents Club", which was a competition amongst the sales reps of the insurance company that he worked. The winners were to receive an all expense paid trip to the Bahamas. This was a six-month competition and at the end of the competition, he had qualified as one of the winners. His time after her abortion was consumed with this competition so his communication with her was minimal and certainly did not include any physical escapades. Roger did tell Delia that he had won an all expense paid trip, for two to the Bahamas after the competition was over. The Insurance Company that he worked for, Penncorp Financial offered this as a bonus once a year to their top grossing sales representatives and Roger was proudly one of them. He had initially asked another young lady to accompany him on this trip that he was at that time dating, but he later had a falling out with her so he had to find another female to take this trip of a lifetime with.

He decided to ask Delia to accompany him and she accepted. Since, he had not seen her in a while and was not serious with anyone in particular the situation seemed ideal. He felt this would be the perfect place for them to reacquaint themselves, with one another.

The day of the flight out, everything was fine. They both were in great spirits. When he picked her up for the drive to the airport, she seemed just as excited as he was. Little did he know, things would change once they made it to their destination.

They anxiously arrived at the hotel, Paradise Island Hotel and Casino, and began to unpack their clothes. The excitement was insurmountable as he gazed almost in a trance at the beautiful surroundings that they were encountering and the prospect of the weekend that the two of them were about to embark on. All of a sudden, Delia became moody and distant. Roger tried to ignore the mood swing hoping this was something that would soon pass and they would have a wonderful time there in the Bahamas.

Then she began to explain to him (and made it quite clear) she was not interested in having sex with him on this trip. In her words, "If that is the reason you brought me with you then you have made a mistake." He was immediately taken by surprise. This had not been a consideration of his at all, however, given their past and the fact that this was a romantic weekend for two; He naturally assumed that they would get to know one another again intimately. He knew it had been months since they were intimate with each other, but he never thought it would be an issue, now. He just simply did not understand why she would accept a trip with him to a place like Paradise Island knowing that she went only for the sake of taking a free trip.

She abruptly tainted the atmosphere with her declaration. Greatly disappointed, he could no longer play along with the "happy couple" role and she knew she could no longer portray that facade, either.

From that point on neither of them enjoyed the weekend. Roger tried because he had friends and co-workers their along with him, but it was extremely difficult. The other couples, who accompanied them on this excursion, were enjoying themselves, cuddled up together pool-side while making jokes of the great times that they themselves were having after "lights out" but all he could think about at that point was getting home.

Her distance with him on this trip simply ruined it and so when they returned to Chicago, he cut off all correspondence with her. He was quite upset and felt she destroyed this trip, purposely. She promised him sex when they returned (for his inconvenience, I guess), as if that would make up for the ruined trip.

Roger was not in the mood to take her up on her offer and decided to keep her at a distance, but he eventually reconciled with her, about the trip to the Bahamas and they saw each other a few times after that. On the last time he saw her, the two had sex, however, when she reached her climax, she pushed him off. Her explanation was that at one time in her life, she had sex to satisfy others, but now she was only interested in satisfying herself. He was infuriated as he left her house to get to his apartment and take a cold shower.

When he looked back in hindsight, he began to believe that Delia may have purposely instigated several situations like this in order to get his attention (or maybe someone else's attention), but it was his attention that she happened to get. He made the decision on that day to leave her alone completely and from that point on; he did not attempt to contact her.

Deceived

It was November 1985, and Roger had not spoken to Delia since July. One evening, when he was home relaxing, the phone rang and to his surprise it was she. He thought that when he cut her off months ago she would get the message and move on. He had no real interest in her; however, he took her call.

This time she revealed to him that she was three months pregnant. According to her, it was not his child. He initially questioned it only because he knew it might be possible. She assured him that it was not his child and he accepted her word. As they talked on, she told him about the difficulty she was having facing her family as a 3-month pregnant woman and Thanksgiving was coming with the prospect of the questions and conversation that she would have with her family at Thanksgiving dinner and because of this, she was going to spend the holiday alone. Roger unthinkingly invited her to have Thanksgiving dinner with he and his family at his mother's home. She was visibly pregnant, so they explained to his family that they were simply friends and the baby she was carrying was not his child.

A month later, in December, she called him and told him that she had an ultrasound and the results were that she was pregnant with twins. She explained how she was wrong about the paternity and that he must be the father because he was a twin, as well. He naively, without question, believed her and accepted his responsibility. It was important to him that he support her and help to raise their child. You would think that by this time he would be running from her; however, his Baptist upbringing and his strong family orientation would not allow him to walk away from the fact that there was a great potential that this child was actually his.

Roger's mother instilled in him at a young age the importance of keeping family together. She was a very protective and proud, Christian woman. She became a widow at a young age and had to raise Roger, his brother, his three sisters, by herself.

His father passed away when he was five years old in 1963 and all he could remember about him was that he was a minister and a tall man who had a profound belief system and was a man of his word. Although his mother was the very best parent anyone could possibly hope for, he himself was a boy who needed the direction of a man so he always felt a void and knew he would never allow his children to know that kind of emptiness.

His mother began keeping other children and foster children, in order to be home with him and his siblings, and raise them up in a proper fashion. This not only supported the family financially, but also gave them the parental support needed through out the days of their young lives. It was because of acts like that, that he and his siblings realized the importance of family through their mother.

She instilled the belief in him that if a child of his was ever conceived out of wedlock, the honorable and right thing to do would be to marry the mother of that child.

He respected his mother's opinions and he remembered as a young man that he had made himself two promises; one, he would not have children with multiple mommies and two, he would not allow a child of his to be born into this world without being married to their mother, just as she had taught him.

Roger went to his mother to tell her the new development of the pregnancy and to find out how she felt. Although, she did not agree with his decision to marry Delia she did support him.

On March 15, 1986, he married Delia. On their drive home from the wedding she, with no shame, said, "I can stop working, now."

Roger, was confused by her statement and he realized a change in atmosphere had come once again. Just like when they were in the Bahamas. She wasted no time dashing his hopes of marital bliss, only this time he knew it was not a three-day trip, but a trip of a lifetime. Naively he thought that he could make it work.

Sometime later in her pregnancy she claimed there would only be one child born. That the doctor told her that she lost one child and the child disintegrated in her womb. He never questioned the legitimacy of her claim and assumed it was possible. He did not attend the doctor's appointment with her and never fathomed she could be misleading him.

Again, I say, naivete played a huge part in this relationship and he, would later be left with doubts of his first child's paternity. Regardless to the air of suspicion, in his heart the child was his. He loved and cherished his time with the child and would be the very best father that he could be to this child.

On May 9, 1986, his first-born, Richard Elijah Scott, made his worldly debut. As Richard crowned and flowed through the birth canal, the nurse handed a pair of scissors to Roger. She tied off the umbilical cord and instructed him on where to cut. The nurse washed up the baby and then handed him to Roger. He looked at him with all the love in his heart, then presented him to his mother.

That was the greatest moment of his life. Nothing in his life had he experienced, up to that point, came close to the feelings that ran through his body and soul at that precise time. He was a father, a dad, a guiding force in life, a very proud and thankful man. *This is my son, my child, my name bearer, my first born, and sure to become my best friend*, he thought to himself. He was so very grateful to God that his child had come into the world in perfect health.

This moment was diminished shortly after Delia was fully coherent. Again, she wasted no time belittling him. In her mind, he had offered her no support. She gave him no credit for his assistance with the birth. According to her, he was absolutely no help in the delivery process and she went through this entire process alone.

He tried desperately to understand her point of view. She was the one experiencing the entire physical trauma that comes with giving birth. How could she deny so easily his contributions to this birth? He did, in fact, attend, complete, and received a certificate for Lamaze classes. He consistently kept a written log of her contractions all night long prior to the delivery. He helped with the breathing techniques during her labor, and administered the ice chips to her lips when she felt dehydrated. It was his strands of hair, in her hands, that she pulled during the culmination of labor pains, while referring to him with names too vulgar to repeat. Yes, he could see her point, his assistance was non-existent, but at least she did not deny his role in naming his son.

He named his son Richard, after his favorite uncle. Roger's uncle was named after his grandfather, a man whom he had never met, but knew of his great contributions to the family. He was a man who served in a long line of ministers in his family.

His Uncle Richard was a Watkins Products door-to-door salesperson. He sold cold remedies and salves. He was also an old Baptist preacher in his hometown of Nashville, Tennessee. Every year when Roger's family had a family reunion in Nashville there was no question where he and his brother, Ricky, would stay. They were young fellas and were crazy about Uncle Richard.

Roger and his brother would hop into the car with Uncle Richard as he would go door to door with his products and call out, "Watkins Man." They were so proud of him and they loved to imitate his call. He and his brother would march around, calling out, "Watkins man,

Watkins man," even when they were back home in Chicago.

He did pretty well selling Watkins remedies because he did that until the day he retired. He remained his favorite up until the day that he died. A good man he was. He was Roger's hero, a father figure and a role model to both he and his brother. He was the man that Roger wanted to be to his children.

The days following Richard's birth were filled with newness. He loved learning to change his diapers, bathe, and dress him. Holding this precious person, and feeling his total dependence on him was a life changing experience. The love he felt for this child from the womb to birth, mere words could never describe. He was his pride and joy, and he alone became the reason for Roger to live his life to the fullest. He wanted to give and share all that he could with this beautiful child. As time went on, he would find out that he did not have that type of control.

Two months after Richard was born, Roger took his new family to the annual family reunion in Nashville, Tennessee. Richard was christened that year at the family reunion and his, eighty-year-old Uncle Richard performed the ceremony at the family reunion. This was a special right of passage and it was made more special because his favorite uncle lived to, and was able to, perform the service himself for his firstborn who was in fact named after him.

The Scott Family Reunions began in about the year of 1940 and took place on the first Sunday of July, every year since. Hosting the reunion rotated between Roger's father's eleven brothers and sisters. The family reunion usually took place in a community center or park field house. The ceremony consisted of a brief gospel service and that year the christening of Richard to kick off the festivities. Then there is the introduction of each of his father's siblings and their families. Artifacts and exhibits from each familial branch are usually displayed. Finally, everyone would enjoy the best home cooked meal you would ever taste in your life. Even though his father was deceased, his mother made sure that he and his siblings attended this reunion year after year. She recognized the importance of the bond and relationship of her children with both sides of the family. Roger wanted to make sure that his son was exposed to this history throughout his life and he prayed Delia seeing his entire family and the roots he came from would help to assure her that he was committed to their new family.

Things were great between Delia and Roger, during the Family Reunion. One morning, while shaving his beard in the hotel room, he cut himself. He touched the cut with his finger and walked into the room where Delia was to show her that he had cut himself.

Delia who was lying across the bed saw the blood roll down his finger. She leaped off the bed and went to her suitcase to retrieve the first aid kit that she had brought in her effort to be prepared for anything. Then she began wiping his finger with a cotton ball soaked with alcohol.

She was so proud of herself for being prepared. Roger tried to stop her, but she just shushed him and began wrapping his finger with a band-aid. When she returned to her place on the bed, he looked at her with amusement and said, "Thank you, but the blood was from my face."

They looked at each other and roared with laughter. That, was one of the few times the two of them would share a smile.

Again his excitement was short-lived. Not long after the trip to Tennessee, Delia began to show her irritable nature. She seemed to have a constant problem with just about anything that he would do. He would just excuse it, believing it was due to post-partum depression.

One evening, Roger was playing with Richard and she said to him, "I can't seem to get you to do anything for me; you are spending all your time with the baby. I don't know why you are eating him up so. He's not yours anyway! Look at him! He has his father's eyes."

For a moment, he was crushed. He stood there paralyzed by those words and in a fit of anger; he turned and started toward her.

She noticed the anger in his eyes as he approached her. Immediately, she began to retract her words, saying, "I'm sorry! I'm sorry! I'm just lying. I only said that to hurt you."

Moreover, hurt him she did. He felt betrayed by those words. He had completely changed the course of his life to accommodate this woman and infant who was supposed to be his child. Was she telling the truth given the circumstances? Nonetheless, when he turned and looked into the eyes of Richard, it did not matter to him at all. *He is mine and I believe it whole-hearted*ly, he thought.

Backing Into Hard Times

Roger had ideas of a life of grandeur, while his wife resented every moment that she spent with him. One Saturday afternoon, Roger's back went out. This was the result of an automobile accident that he had about six years prior. Periodically, the problem would flare up, making it very difficult to move. In order to get relief, all he could do was lie in bed consumed with the pain in his back.

He asked Delia to get some ointment out of the medicine cabinet and rub it on his back. She proceeded to the bathroom, got the ointment, handed it to him, and then walked away.

He could not believe her. She did not assist him in any way. He lay there, helpless, with the tube of ointment in his hand. Did she expect him to rub this on his own back?

He was in too much pain to question her and surely was not ready for an argument. Instead, he struggled to the phone, called his sister, Trina, and asked her to pick him up.

She came right away, took him to her house, and

assisted Roger with a muscle relaxer and pain medication until he was well enough to go home and get back to work.

Life at home was difficult, to say the least. Delia raised hell daily, constantly complaining. His only motivation for returning home each evening was Richard. He would spend as little time as possible under the same roof with her. At this point, Roger was working as Marketing Director at the Insurance Exchange, which was a newly-formed insurance group located in the suburbs of Chicago. He also took part-time employment on the staff of one of Chicago's city council members. His duties there was to assist within the sixth ward, anything that the alderman might need be it precinct work or door to door passing out information from the aldermanic office.

Practically living out of his car, you could find fast food cups, bags, and wrappers everywhere. Starting his days early and ending late became his lifestyle, he would find one more customer to visit with and one more client he needed to add to his roster each evening just to keep from making it home while she was awake.

This was the first year of their marriage and maybe they were just experiencing growing pains. It was a lot for the two of them to absorb in such a short time.

Richard was a ball of energy. He was a delightful and fun-filled child. Roger loved this child with all of his heart and soul and Richard became the one and only reason for him to stay with this woman. He spent the better part of his first one and a half years loving him.

Delia was pregnant with their second child at this point and he was hoping this would make the relationship stronger. Exactly one year and six months after the birth of Richard, their second child was born. Aaron DeAndre Scott made his debut November 9, 1987. With his birth, Roger was also in the delivery room, assisting Delia, cutting the umbilical cord, and bonding with him.

Roger looked at the newborn and said, "This is a funny-looking child."

One of the attending nurses replied, "I don't know what you are talking about. He looks exactly like you."

He smiled as he watched him and again his heart filled with an over whelming sense of pride and joy. He looked forward to having a junior.

After the baby's birth, when he and his mom were settled, Roger went home to take care of Richard. When he returned to the hospital the next morning, to his surprise and dismay, she had taken it upon herself to name him Aaron, despite his reservations.

What a blow…he sincerely looked forward to having him named after himself. This meant the world to him, but he could do nothing about it. Roger wrapped himself up emotionally with the children and stayed dedicated to his decision never to leave them.

On November 27, 1987, just two weeks after Aaron's birth, tragedy struck the City of Chicago. The beloved mayor, Harold Washington, died in his office. Harold Washington was the first African American to serve as mayor of the City of Chicago. The presiding Alderman, whose staff Roger was a member of, was in line to become the successor. The weeks following the mayor's death were consumed with meetings at city hall in an effort to garner enough votes, for the alderman to be voted Acting Mayor and finish out the term of this great man.

He relinquished his position with the Insurance Exchange Company and made himself completely available for a position on the staff of the next mayor. After a heated debate, one late night, in the City Council Chamber, his boss was elected by a majority vote to complete the term of Harold Washington.

Working in the initial days of transition within the Mayor's office, his time at home became increasingly and now legitimately limited. Knowing Delia was home with both the newborn and their one-and-a-half-year-old, he felt a little guilty about his absence. He wanted to show her his gratitude and let her know that he was thinking of her and decided to surprise her with flowers from the mayor's office one afternoon.

That evening, when he made it home, he cautiously looked around for the floral arrangement that he had sent to her. When he did not see it, he asked her if she received the flowers earlier that day. She said yes. Roger smiled and asked where the flowers were.

She replied, "You didn't have to pay for them and I threw them away." He was speechless. She assumed because the message stated they were from the mayor's office that he did not actually pay for the flowers. Little did she know he did indeed pay for the arrangement out of his own pocket. What difference did it make, he thought. It was the thought that really should have been the only thing that mattered.

He simply did not understand what he was doing wrong. It came to his attention that no matter what he did, he would not be able to please this woman.

The Family Man

Roger's mother was licensed by the State of Illinois to keep children and she served as the children's baby sitter during the day while he worked. She kept Richard so that his wife could tend to the newborn during the day, with as little anxiety as possible.

One Friday before he left for work, Delia asked Roger if he could assist her on Saturday. She wanted him to get the children's clothes ready for church for the following Sunday. He agreed to do so.

He worked all day Saturday in the mayor's office. His boss, the former alderman was now the acting mayor. That evening, he returned home and immediately began to start getting things together for church on Sunday. Once Delia realized what he was doing, she informed him that it had already been done. She said to him that his assistance was not necessary she had done it herself. He stopped what he was doing, cooked and ate dinner, then went to bed.

On Sunday, Roger got up early, took a shower, and began getting dressed for church. Before he could realize her resentment toward him, she asked him if he thought the only responsibility he had was to get ready. He replied, "No." He definitely knew that he had a responsibility to the children to help get them dressed and he did the best that he could to do just that.

He explained that his plan was to shower, dress, then feed and dress Richard. He assumed that she would handle the baby and herself because he was about five weeks old. He cooked breakfast and began dressing Richard.

Then she said to him, "Now you are going to take things over after I got their clothes ready."

Roger asked her, "What do you want me to do?"

She replied, "Leave. Get your clothes and things and go I don't want you here."

He did not see this coming. This was a wonderful way to start a Sunday morning. He was still cognizant of the possibility that she may be suffering from post-partum depression just as she did with Richard and he felt she did not mean what she was saying. Therefore, he decided that he would dress Richard and take him to his mother's house for a few hours. Maybe some time alone would give her a break from the toddler and time to realize what she was saying.

As Roger began to dress Richard, she came over to him and began removing his clothing. He tried putting the clothes back on and she proceeded to take them off, again.

He asked, "What's going on here, Delia?"

She answered, "Dress him in something you paid for, don't put him in anything I paid for."

Roger was momentarily at a loss for words. What was wrong with this woman? What exactly had he done wrong this time?

Let me check. He woke up, got dressed, started getting the oldest child ready…hmmm, can't think of anything that could have set her off this way.

"Leave, and take your clothes with you," she yelled.

At this point, he left Richard where he was and began to fill garbage bags with his clothes. As he filled the bags, she would pick them up and empty them in the middle of the bed. He would grab the garbage bags from her and began filling them again.

He started to believe that she really did not want him to leave, but she continued yelling and screaming at him. Then she grabbed a pot, filled it with water and grits and put it on the stove to boil.

Shaking and nervous from the confrontation, he sped up the packing. He was almost done getting his clothes together when she picked the pot up off the stove and emptied it in his direction. She soaked his suits, his clothes, and got some of the hot water on him.

Now, Roger was fuming and, without thinking, he slapped her. For the first time in his life, he actually hit a member of the opposite sex. He paused in disgrace, hurt and angered with himself and totally confused about how things could have reached this level. This was done by reaction and he had not in any way allowed anyone else to push him that far.

Delia ran downstairs to the apartment occupied by her sister and had her to take a picture of her face. Then she called the Chicago Police.

When the police arrived, she told them Roger had hit her and she wanted him out of her house. Roger explained to the police that he was trying to get his things and leave when she threw a pot of boiling grits at him. The police asked her if she was pressing charges and, to his surprise, she said no and went on to tell the police that he was an employee of the mayor and that pressing charges would not do any good.

The police told Roger to leave and give her time to cool off. Worried that she might try something else, he asked them to stay until he gathered all of his clothing. He wanted to make sure that when he left that he would not have to return. They stayed until he finished and Roger was thankful.

It was a little more than a month after Aaron's birth that Roger actually left her. Both children were too young to remember him living in the same household with them. He wanted them to know that he did not just walk away from them. He longed to be there with them, but at that point he was sure if he remained there, someone could possibly be hurt physically.

The Court Fight

Roger moved back into his mother's house until he could find himself an apartment. In the meantime, Delia decided that she would no longer bring the children to his mother's house for babysitting. He assumed that it was because he was living there and she did not want him to have any contact with the children.

She then arranged for her mother to keep their children. Shortly thereafter, he received a summons to appear in court. She had filed for divorce. Roger was shaken. This came after less than two years of their marriage.

He always believed that marriages broke up based on trust, financial, and infidelity issues, but could not believe she was willing to give up this relationship and the things they could have built together over this incident. Although he experienced the brunt of her anger and obvious misery, he still attributed it to post-partum depression. He still was willing to work it out for the sake of the children, but the summons made it clear her feelings were not reciprocal.

During the first few weeks of working in the mayor's office, the new acting mayor received visitors from across the country. One of these visitors was Ms. Correta Scott-King, the wife of the late Dr. Martin Luther King Jr. Roger was in and out of court with his soon-to-be ex-wife that day and it was taking its toll on him. He had no idea if this was showing on his face or if Ms. King simply had the intuition. However, she was standing outside of city hall on LaSalle Street, and Roger came out of the building. She turned and looked at him as he approached her she said to him, "Young man, something is bothering you, and whatever it is just know that this, too, shall pass."

Roger was completely blown away. This great woman, for whatever reason, had stopped to give him a word of encouragement. How could she possibly know? What she did not know was that her words would be with him for the rest of his life. She made such an impact on him, without even knowing what the situation was. She, alone, gave Roger the strength to realize he could withstand any and everything that may come his way and he now knew he would never give up.

Always having to make things difficult, Delia would not agree to the terms of the divorce. The two of them ended up spending two years in a court, hammering out the terms of custody. He would give her whatever she wanted as long as he could have fair opportunity in the lives of the children. What she wanted was for him to pay her for a vehicle that he was driving, despite the fact that the car had been paid for and it was Roger who made the monthly payments on it prior to their divorce. She also wanted him to pay her mother an additional $2,700.00. His mother-in-law claimed that he owed her money for babysitting at the rate of $50.00 per week for one year. She did this because he had given her mother a money order for $100.00 that first week that Delia had taken the children to her to care for when, in fact, Roger's mother had been the babysitter prior to the divorce proceedings. He never arranged with her mother to keep the children and what's more, he never agreed to pay her $50.00 per week. The court decided that since he had given her $100.00 then there was an unspoken agreement to pay her regularly. These two financial issues were given to Roger as arrearages and were to be satisfied by paying an additional amount to his bi-weekly child support. What was not clear was the definition of child support because if he was, in fact, meeting his child support orders then the money that was designated for support should have been used to satisfy the babysitting charges that he was being held responsible for. What exactly is child support supposed to be used for? This is a question that, even today, there are no answers for, because Delia has told him constantly over the years that he did not buy any of the children's clothes or pay any of her bills and that he was, in fact, a "deadbeat dad." This she told him even though he paid child support and his support was paid regularly to his estranged wife.

According, to the agreement Roger would have the children three days and three nights and she would have them four days and four nights every week. During this time, Roger was appointed assistant to the first deputy commissioner in the Department of Aviation in Chicago. His office was located at O'Hare Airport and he was beginning to feel as if his star was beginning to rise as far as his career was concerned; however, the distraction of the divorce proceedings and the prospect of not sharing these successes with his family made his career somewhat bittersweet. His salary dictated that the child support that the children were entitled to well exceeded the needs of children who were one and two years old at that time. The big question now, given the visitation arrangement that they were given sharing the children on an almost equal basis, why was child support levied at the rate that it was by the judicial system? Today, the child support system has been utilized by the state as a method of welfare reform. Parents are ostracized from the lives of their children for the sole purpose of the state making money from its child support collection procedures. The court has taken the position of putting parents in a position of little or no contact with their children and levying insurmountable child support orders to justify the non-contact orders that are given. The states have created agencies whose sole purpose is to collect child support by any means necessary. There are currently no created agencies that exist that perpetuates ongoing relationships with children by both parents which would indeed recognize that each child has a God given right to enjoy a quality relationship with both parents whether that parent resides in the same household with them or not. These same state agencies are making millions of dollars annually by charging each parent who pays support to their children. Our society has made in effect, cash cows, of parents while the courts have destroyed the lives and relationships of countless parents. After the initial court date, for the divorce proceedings, the bailiff in the court room, where the case was being heard, followed Roger out of the court room and pulled him to the side and said," son, I can see that you are trying to do the right thing with your life but, I just wanted you to know that I feel sorry for you." At this point, he had no idea what he meant.

After a couple of years in the position of Assistant to the First Deputy Commissioner in the Department of Aviation, a special election was held and Roger lost his position because the mayor was not reelected. He was now in the uncomfortable position of owing child support in an amount that was calculated based on the salary of the job that he had just lost. Once again, he had to pay an attorney to file a motion for a reduction in child support, even though his children were with him almost half of each week.

After losing that position, his sister, who also lost a position as Assistant Commissioner in the Department of Water for the City of Chicago, and he opened a lounge on 84th and South Chicago Avenue, called The Cozy N, located on the south side of the city, and the two of them began to build this business.

Shortly after Delia realized the lounge was open, she began making complaints about the lounge to the Chicago Police. She would send them to the lounge on the busiest nights with complaints about anything. This was all done in an effort to have the business shut down. Roger did not understand this logic because the child support that he was paying to her was coming from his salary in the business that she was trying so hard to have closed.

One evening after closing the lounge for the night, Roger and his sister stopped in at another lounge, just to listen to music and unwind. While there, the lounge owner approached them and began explaining the details of an open meeting, held sometime prior, with an alderman within the city. He continued to tell about a young woman named Ms. Lang-Street. Well, her name was not Lang-Street. It was Lang-Scott, Roger's ex wife. She had addressed the alderman and the other officials about their lounge.

He claimed that she stated that she wanted to have the lounge closed. According to him, the alderman of that particular ward that the lounge she spoke of was not in his jurisdiction. However, when asked why she wanted the lounge closed she explained that her ex-husband and his sister owned the club and were selling alcohol to minors.

Roger found the story and the situation she put herself in to be absurd. It explained why many evenings the Chicago police would come into the lounge, during the busiest hours checking the patrons' identifications. The police would always explain to that they were receiving reports that they were serving alcohol to minors. The police never found any evidence or any reason to believe so, except the anonymous reports.

Roger knew and felt it was she from the start and found it outrageous that she would spend her personal time plotting ways to destroy him financially. It was as if she spent every moment of spare time that she had doing this. He always wondered what affect it might be having on the children. He would later find out the painful truth.

Once she told him, "Fathers are not important," and her only concern was with how much child support she would get and how little time with the boys Roger would get. She was, obviously determined to make him pay as much as possible. Roger had no problem paying as much as they needed and deserved. If he could not be in the home to help her raise them, the least that he could do was to make sure that he provided for them financially. His only problem was getting the quality time he deserved. At this time, The Oprah Winfrey Show was doing a series on alimony and child support. Roger attended two of her tapings and was chosen to speak from the studio audience on one show where he addressed the issue of alimony with the couple who were being featured on her show. He later found out that Delia told his children that he was on Oprah and that he talked about her, which gave her more reason to frustrate his visitation orders as much as she could while also giving the children the idea that he actually embarrassed her publicly.

Delia continued to frustrate his visitation. This was only the beginning of the nightmare that she would inflict on Roger's entire family. She would ignore the fact that there were court orders in place specifically stating his visitation. He would go to the house to pick them up and she would not answer the door. Discouraged, he would leave and return with the police to enforce his court orders, which were not enforceable by the police.

Their custody arrangement stated that Roger would be privy to all records from school, dental and doctors' records, and any other activity that the children were a part of, as well. Delia worked for the school they eventually attended and she put a stop to all communication between the school and him.

Once the boys started school, the schools were aware of the joint custody agreement. They would send him notices of PTA meetings, and their grades. He tried to be involved in as many aspects of their lives as possible. He felt children needed to know that both parents would be there for them and would support all their efforts.

One evening, after attending a PTA meeting with Richard, who was about five years old at the time and full of energy and just a ball of lightning, the two of them were walking through the corridor of the school on their way to the car when they noticed the maintenance man who was still working. Richard called out his name and took off running toward him. When he got to him, Richard hugged his leg. Surprised and confused, Roger grabbed Richard and apologized to the maintenance worker. He had never seen this man in his life and assumed Richard knew him because his mother worked there at the school and he must have been acquainted with him through her, but felt seeing him did not grant that type of a response.

Roger explained to Richard on the ride home that his hugs should be reserved for Mommy, Daddy, Grandmother, Grandfather and his aunts and uncles. When he dropped Richard off to his mother, he brought up this incident. He questioned Richard's fondness for the man. She made it clear that it was her position that it was okay for the children to be loving to all people and she taught this to them. Roger was utterly upset and told her that she should not condone these children expressing affection with anyone other than their family because strangers often took advantage of small children.

Allegations of Molestation

A few years later, Roger remarried and in the back of his mind, he would eventually file for custody of the boys because he would have been fair with the distribution of their time and he felt that boys need to have a strong male figure in their lives. One Labor Day weekend, the first weekend of his visitation with the boys after remarriage, he drove the boys to his aunt's bed and breakfast in Union Pier, Michigan. It was a tourist home, which was about an hour outside of Chicago. They all spent the day playing in the yard with family and barbecuing.

As it got late, Roger ask his mother to drive the boys back to Chicago and he would pick them up the following morning. He needed to get back to the lounge in order to tend to the Saturday night crowd. That night, Roger's nephew, who was fifteen years old at the time, rode back with him so that he could help with the clean up of the lounge, after closing.

When he picked the boys up from his mother's house that Sunday morning, he also had to drop his nephew off there. It was a short exchange as Roger helped his mother gather the boys' things and the three headed to his apartment where they spent the remainder of the day. He dropped the children off at their mother's house later that evening.

When he returned to pick them up on the next scheduled visitation, which was a few days later, Delia told him that the Department of Children and Family Services had advised her not to allow the children to come into his custody. They were investigating a child molestation charge she had filed with the Chicago Police. She named his nephew as the alleged perpetrator in the case.

Roger could not believe his ears. He knew that his nephew could not have committed this crime because he had been with him and he felt this was another one of her plots to hurt him.

According to the charges she filed, his nephew fondled the children and masturbated on them. This began a chain of events that went through the Department of Children and Family Services, to the Chicago Police who did an investigation and were going to charge Roger's nephew as an adult because he was going to turn sixteen in December.

When Roger asked Delia what she had to substantiate her claims, she told him that she had the children checked by a physician who found evidence and verified her claims. Immediately, he went to visit the physician who checked the boys. When he asked if he could view the physician's findings and see for himself, the physician emphatically denied access to their records. He stated that Delia had instructed him not to allow access because she was pursuing charges of child molestation and that

Roger was involved. Roger went back home to obtain his court orders, which specifically stated that he was privy to all medical records. He returned to the physician's office and showed him the court orders, but it was only after he threatened to call the police, that he was allowed to have a look at their medical records.

Their records confirmed the boys had been in to see their physician recently. It explained their current physicals, which included a recent updating of their normal vaccinations. There was no mention of trauma nor evidence or mention that molestation had taken place at any time with either of the boys. In fact, their visit to the doctor was based only on the need for them to have their shots before school began that September.

During this time, the courts would not allow the children to visit his mother's home because part of her claim was that the molestation took place at her house. So now the children were banned from visiting their paternal grandmother.

It took a couple of years and exoneration of these trumped up charges before the children could actually visit their grandmother at her house again.

Soon after, Delia stopped all of the notification that Roger was receiving from the school concerning the children. This was only the first of many actions she took to keep him uninformed of their educational progress.

Roger later found out that she removed his name from their records as an emergency contact or for anything else. Her explanation to Roger was that if the school knew that he was involved with the children then their tuition would go up. What Roger did not understand was why the school would increase their tuition simply because he was involved, when their court orders specifically stated upon her request that she would take responsibility of their school fees and Roger would handle their college education.

She kept their doctor's records away from him and everything else she could think of. She never even informed him of what doctor she was now taking them to and simply refused to give him that information. She told Roger that she was going to make sure the children did not trust him and would make sure they hated him. He could not believe she would go to such lengths to keep these children away from their father.

Delia and Roger were ordered by the court to attend therapy with the children after the charges of molestation. Roger was content in joining the sessions and wanted to put this lie to rest. These events took a major toll on his new marriage. Upon ending the therapy sessions, the Psychologist stated that he could not find any evidence of molestation, but that the children had indeed suffered some type of trauma, but could not relate this trauma to molestation.

It was in the psychologist waiting room when Roger heard her say to the children, "Your father doesn't care about you because he doesn't believe that his nephew did these things to you. He is taking the side of the person that hurt you and if he cared he would be on your side." She went on to tell them that he was not a good father. Roger ignored statements like that and never defended himself to the boys because he felt that the children themselves would see over time that he was indeed a good dad and that he loved them both with all of his heart. Today, neither of the boys can remember anything that Roger's nephew supposedly did to them and they have never said that anything did happen to them to Roger. She would do anything and everything to turn these children against him.

Finally, the police investigators and the Children and Family Services Department could not find any evidence to support her claim. After the investigation, the Chicago Police called the charges unfounded but the Department of Children and Family Services left the charges (as indicated) on his nephew's record. This put his nephew in a position where he can never work around children for the rest of his life. He was sixteen years old at that time, never convicted of the crime and never completely exonerated either. Just to give you an idea of the ineptness of the system with charges as serious as this, Roger wrote a letter to the Department of Children and Family Services (DCFS), which included the findings of the Chicago Police Department and asked them to remove the indicated status from his nephew's. After six months, he received a letter from DCFS stating that because he was not a parent of the alleged perpetrator and the children in question were not in his custody then they could neither make any changes nor give him any information of this particular case. There was no punishment for her for filing a false report nor did she regret one moment that she had spent turning everyone's life upside down. Delia used Roger's nephew as a pawn, a sacrificial lamb to drive him out of the lives of his children, but it did not work. It made him work more diligently and harder to maintain his presence. She jeopardized a young boy's freedom because of her attitude.

Her teaching of the children was becoming evident. The Oprah Winfrey Show did one of its shows at the school that the children attended. This particular show was about working mothers and its effect on children. Six-year-old Aaron was chosen as one of the children who Oprah interviewed and asked the question, "How do you feel about your mom working."

Aaron replied, "I wish my mom didn't have to work so much...maybe for one day... for like one minute." Somehow, even the youngest child had been taught that mothers are supposed to be taken care of and not have to work for a living.

After the molestation charge, she stepped up her efforts to keep the children from Roger and began to reject his visitation even more. Because of the molestation charges against his nephew, and the change in the visitation by the court system, she felt that she had gained some power or momentum in her quest to downplay his significance with the boys. She was now able to deny access to the boys. Roger came by to pick the boys up on a warm summer Saturday morning and heard her voice inside, saying, "Get down." This he heard through an open window. The car was in the driveway, the windows are open on the first floor yet no one answered the doorbell when he rang. This, he found out later was a game that she told them to play with Roger (hide and seek from daddy). They were too young to realize what she was actually doing and played along. She was able to do this and get away with it because the courts did not favor Roger visiting the boys because of the trumped up charges of his nephew. Even after the charges were unfounded and he was granted visitation, it was at a much-reduced rate than it had been prior.

The divorce proceedings took two years and cost $20,000 before it was over. It was, prolonged simply because of Roger's fight for shared parenting which at that time was a very hard thing to get within the court system. He was eventually granted joint custody although it meant nothing to her and was only as good as the paper it was written on because at that time there was no legal mechanism in place to enforce a custody agreement. The attorney that was chosen was a documented father's rights advocate who advertised himself as an attorney on the side of fathers to get quality time with their children. However, the initial visit to the attorney was scheduled after Roger could provide him with a retainer, in the amount of, $3,500.00, which was to be paid by either cash or certified check. That retainer was exhausted within three months when Roger began receiving bills from his attorney outlining charges for telephone calls or any other movement in his fight for shared parenting. Between the attorney fees, child support and his normal living expenses, Roger had to let the attorney go and complete the divorce Pro Se. This was a major disappointment. Finding that an attorney, who prides himself on the rights of fathers and champions himself as the answer to the problems that non custodial parents face, was actually, simply one of those who was cashing in on the emotional hurt and pain and distress of parents who want nothing more than a relationship with their children.

The divorce proceedings ended and Roger was granted the divorce on his birthday, exactly two years after it had begun. This process cost so much money and took so much out of him emotionally, physically, and spiritually that he began to cry on the el train while riding home from the court on the day the divorce was final. He was so overwhelmed that he just sat in one of the seats and began crying uncontrollably. He did not care if anyone was watching him. The tears were beyond attention seeking, beyond selfish satisfaction and beyond what anyone could understand. He was crying because he felt that this nightmare had finally ended. He was literally exhausted. Delia had begun to break his spirit. Roger wiped his eyes and as he rode and thought about the entire ordeal that he had gone through, He began to remember those precious and encouraging words Ms. King said to him previously, "Whatever it is, this too shall pass." Those words haunted him because he knew she was right and that one day all of what he had been through would be well worth it to his children. Roger knew that he could sit back and just allow the chips to fall where they may or he could fight it through and work to try to make the chips fall the right way where he too would have a parental relationship with his children.

As it would be, this was only the end of the marriage, but not the end of the games and vicious attacks.

Initially, Roger's half of the custody consisted of having the boys every day of the week after school until 8:00 p.m. He returned them to their mother on the days they were to spend the night with her. They were to spend the night with him three nights a week and the only time that he was not supposed to be with them were the second and fourth weekends. This custody arrangement came with the normal status quo award of child support to her, taking no consideration of the fact that the children were ordered to be with him substantially. After the allegations of molestation took place, the orders were modified to reflect that visitation would be on the first and third weekends of every month only, with alternating birthdays, father's day, and his own birthday, along with alternating years on the children's birthdays. It was never restored to its original status, which should have happened automatically when the charges were unfounded. Even this new visitation schedule never happened. Several times, he would have to take the Chicago Police along with his orders to her house during visitation and she still refused to let them come out of the house on occasion. She would tell the boys that Roger was trying to get her put in jail, giving them the idea that she was being mistreated. She would never allow them to bring a change of clothes with them when she did allow them to visit, forcing Roger not only to pay child support, but also to pay for clothing while they were there. The clothing would get little use because it was not often that they got a chance to wear them and they would outgrow the clothes with them hardly being worn.

Finally, Roger was fed up with the way she was treating him. He wrote a letter to the Chicago Sun-Times newspaper. The newspaper published it and he began receiving phone calls from across the country. He found that there were fathers who were experiencing the exact same treatment from their former spouses. The phone calls gave him the understanding that his problems were not isolated problems and he realized that fathers needed support and help all over the United States. This is why he organized and started the non-profit organization Children Need Both Parents, Inc.

His goals, initially, were to assist fathers who have a desire to spend quality time and be a significant part in the lives of their children. Although Delia knew of the project, she did not stop with her objective. His visitation amounted to less than two years of their lives overall. As he calculated the three days monthly that the courts allowed visitation throughout their lifetime and she frustrated most of that time you can very well see that the three of them, Roger, Richard and Aaron have been cheated of the most important relationships in life and that is the relationship between children and their parents. In an effort to further discredit Roger with the children, she would tell the boys that he was coming to pick them up during times when he was not suppose to and they would look for me and their father who would never show. This, she did trying to destroy the trust they had in Roger. Hoping they would not want to be with him when I did show up. The three of them never shared holidays. Delia would, conveniently disappear on holidays and birthdays. Roger told her that she would regret what she was attempting to do and that it would someday come back to haunt her, because the children would someday know the truth but it did not stop her.

Our Precious Time Together

Visiting with the boys was always the highlight of Rogers's existence. He made every minute that he had with them count. They would attend baseball games, go-cart racing and a host of other activities. They prayed, played games, and listened to music together. The three of them made it a ritual to go to a Giordano's Pizzeria in Hyde Park in Chicago and celebrate their birthdays there every year. On the weekend that Roger had visitation following one of their birthdays, he would permit the birthday boy to order whatever he wanted at Giordano's. They tried to sit at the same table every year that they went. You could hear the three of them laughing and telling jokes and simply acting crazy together, celebrating the birthday of one of the children. Roger really wanted to preserve each visit, not knowing when they would have another chance like this.

They would spend the other times at his apartment cooking and enjoying each other's company, to the utmost. The children's weekends with their father were just that and Roger never allowed anyone or anything to intrude on his time with the children. He kept cupcakes, cookies and candy bars in a glass blocked window in the kitchen. The window was so high the children would need a chair to get to it. This they called *the snack window*.

Roger would allow them a snack occasionally and it would tickle him pink to find them sneaking past his bedroom door after bedtime. They thought that their father was sound asleep in his room and they would peek into the room to make sure. Roger, with one eye open and the other closed, would be watching them the entire time, lying there in the dark so they had no idea that they were being watched, as he would smile to himself. The boys would tiptoe into the kitchen to steal a snack or two, and take them back to their bedroom, then fall asleep watching television as they ate the treats. He never said anything to them about it and it actually amused him to know they thought they were pulling one over on their father. The snacks were there for them in the first place.

Roger had a wonderful time whenever the children were with him. Each Christmas season he would wait until the boys arrived to buy and decorate the Christmas tree. He refused to buy or put even one ornament on a tree until they were there. He did not allow anything to come between he and the boys.

It began to occur to him that maybe the boys were realizing their mother was misleading them and beginning to understand that their father was not the man their mom made him out to be. Roger would find out later just how wrong he was. As the boys grew older, they began to layer their clothes in order to give themselves a change of clothing for their visits. They knew that their father washed the clothing they wore when they arrived, every weekend, and returned them clean and neat to their mother without sending any of the clothing he had bought. They realized the clothes that Roger had would not fit, most likely, at their next visit because the visits were so infrequent and the children were growing like weeds.

When Richard was about ten years old, he and Roger began to empty a coffee can that he kept in one of his drawers, filled with receipts for child support, that had sent to their mother prior to an actual judgment for child support. He went through the coffee can and they counted the amount of money together that he had sent to her before it was automatically taken from his paycheck. They counted about $10,000 dollars in money order receipts.

Richard looked at his father and said, "Dad, I am a little confused." He went on to say, "Everyone keeps talking about what you don't do, but you have proof."

This startled Roger. What exactly did he mean when he said everyone? He later found out that she told her family that she did not get money from their father regularly and when she did receive something from him that it was insufficient to her needs, which caused her entire family to resent Roger and actually some of her family members would talk about him negatively to his children.

Roger could not believe this, especially coming from a woman who would not even allow them to bring an overnight bag when they came to spend the night.

However, they were allowed to take an overnight bag with them to spend the night with her relatives.

He decided that the boys could use an allowance because they were nine and ten and needed money of their own. So he began to give them an allowance on the weeks that they were with him. About three months after this began the boys said to their father one weekend that their maternal grandmother had told them that she would give them an allowance so they did not need to take anything from him. It appeared that her family supported this alienation.

The only refuge that he had was to hire another lawyer and go into court to charge her with visitation violations, which would keep him spending money that he did not have.

He felt there were no boundaries with this woman, but what she did not recognize was that his determination exceeded hers. Roger was determined to have a quality relationship with his children at all cost and the memory of the words of Ms. Coretta Scott King would compel him to make it through this time.

As the years past, Roger learned that she talked about him negatively to the children on a constant basis and whenever they spoke to each other, she would talk to him as if I were a villain, even while the children were present. He endured her cursing him out, calling him unspeakable names and just yelling at him when the moment would suit her. Roger, in turn made it a point never to match words with her nor speak to her negatively around the children.

The children would look sad and confused and he would explain some of these incidences as, "Mommy is having a bad day." At times, she would threaten to call the police if he didn't leave, although he would be there to pick up the boys for the weekend. They were not allowed to give their father any of their school pictures and, subsequently, he never received any school pictures of them growing up. They were instructed not to tell their father about events that were taking place because she told the children that she would inform him, which she never did so the children would be disappointed when they were in activities as they grew up and their father was never there. Not because he would not have been, but because he was never told what was taking place until either it was over or it was too late to attend. These things can never be replaced. No amount of money could ever compensate for the events and time lost because of alienation and a lack of the current judicial system to recognize both parents as primary in the lives of children.

One Sunday afternoon, the boys and Roger were deciding what to cook and eat for dinner. The youngest son, Aaron, asked, "Is there anymore fried chicken left from yesterday?"

Roger said to him, "I never cook any more chicken than I am going to eat because I do not like the taste of reheated chicken."

Richard, the oldest son, immediately replied, "Oh yes, Dad, oh yes, I know I am your son because I don't like reheated chicken, either."

A red flag went up in Roger's mind. What made him feel otherwise? How did he relate his paternity to the like or dislike of reheated chicken? Was it just a figure of speech? No, it was not. What he would find out from them next, absolutely floored him. When their mother would get upset with them, she would say to them things such as, "I am sorry that you were ever born." This she would say to Aaron, but to Richard she would say, "Your father isn't your father." How could she be this cruel? How could a loving parent make a statement to a child about his or her father of this magnitude? This is nothing short of mental cruelty. How does a derogatory statement such as this affect a child later on in life? Roger thought that she reserved statements like that for only him and he could handle them, but intentionally saying something like that to a child could destroy them. He knew that what they said, she had said, was in fact true because she has made some of those exact same statements to him.

It hurt Roger to find out what she was saying to them and especially to Richard. If there was a question of paternity, he did not acknowledge it. Roger made no difference in the relationships he had with either of these children and he was hopelessly in love with the both of them because they both belong to him. At the age of fifteen, Richard and his father had a conversation while driving one day about his paternity. Richard explained to his father in depth the statements that his mother makes about his not being his child biologically and Richard expressed to Roger as he explained, "Dad, it doesn't matter what she says. You are my father."

Roger looked at him with nothing but love. He continued to pay his child support for both of them and continue to be the best dad that he could to his children.

He simply could not afford to constantly hire an attorney and go into court. There are many fathers not willing to pay child support or even pay it on time and they run the risk of incarceration. However, when a custodial parent violates court orders, the non-custodial parent must file a motion to go back into court to put this in front of another judge while paying child support, lawyer fees and court cost. This did no good because she would still handle things on her terms.

Whenever visitation time would end and it was time for Roger to drop the boys off at their mother's house, they would always depart with a kiss on the cheek and the words, "I Love You."

The Child Support Dilemma

Roger began working for an organization called, Community Mental Health Council, which was a non-profit organization located in Chicago. This he began when the children had just begun to attend school. His initial position was as an intake therapist. He later transferred to its residential facilities and worked as a mental health professional.

This organization was at one time short of staff members so Roger began to work two full-time shifts for this organization and was making two full-time paychecks. His employer would take out the percentage of child support from the lump sum of the paycheck despite the fact that it was from two distinct full time positions. Consequently, they would send Delia twice as much support as had been ordered. This continued for about two years until his employer realized that the law only provides support from one full time job only. An order was sent to his employer limiting the support amount to a specific number and Roger immediately received a phone call from Delia, saying please call Human Resources and tell them not to cut it down, he found this a bit amusing, given the way that she had been treating him.

Roger's take home pay from his primary source of income after all of the deductions amounted to $297.00 every two weeks. He took a second full-time job, which the courts would inadvertently send a support order to in an effort to collect twice the child support that was already being satisfied from his first job. His days would overlap between the two jobs, which had him working, in effect, six days a week either at night or during the day. On the days that he was scheduled to pick them up, he was met either with resistance or with a tremendously bad attitude from their mother simply because he was there.

Although Roger provided medical insurance and insurance cards for the boys, she never used it. This she did so that he would not know who their doctor was. In fact, she carried insurance on her job for them because it did not cost her anything and it kept him out of their medical records. Roger discovered that she carried this insurance after receiving the wrong medical cards from the insurance company in the mail. These medical cards looked exactly like the ones that he was expecting but they had Delia's social security number on them. He found out that she carried the exact same insurance with the same company. He was carrying the boys on his insurance, as ordered by the court. The company accidentally sent her medical cards to his house. How surprised Roger was to find out after calling the insurance company that she was also carrying medical insurance on the boys and they had two health policies that were identical. She was not utilizing his insurance and allowing him to pay an additional $100.00 monthly for insurance that the children would never use.

There were times when she would choose the most expensive activities to enroll the children in, summer camps without the benefit of even letting Roger know that she was even thinking about enrolling the children. The two of them were ordered to split the cost of the summer camps but the orders also stipulated that they choose these places together taking into consideration the ability to afford them. Nonetheless, she enrolled them and told him how much he owed her. Roger continued to feel she was intentionally trying to exhaust his financial resources in order to see him give up.

After the two years that the divorce proceeding took and paying attorneys up to $200.00 per hour. The combination of this and his family obligations threatened to take him under financially. Roger had no choice other than to work two full time jobs. He stopped working the two shifts at the Community Mental Health Council because they hired staff to take the second shift that he was working. He then took a second position as a psychiatric rehabilitation therapist for another mental health organization. He would begin working at midnight in a mental health crisis facility, go home at 5:00 a.m. spend an hour changing clothes and preparing lunch for the day and return to finish his shift. He would leave this employer and go to another from 8:30 a.m. to 5:00 p.m. Working six days a week and juggling his visitation and his work schedule with coworkers who would take a shift for him on the weekends that the children there. This went on for thirteen years. Not only was he being cheated out of daily contact with the children, he was also cheated out of a normal life.

Normal conversations with their mother were completely out of the realm of reality. Roger was constantly told how irresponsible and inept he was as a financial provider for the children because she felt that the ordered child support was insufficient. "You should be ashamed of yourself," she would say. "I believe that I should be receiving $2,000 monthly for the children. You are not a man. You should not even want to see the children because you are not doing what you should for them."

Roger did everything that he could. Picking them up with no overnight bag caused him to buy them clothing for their visits with him as well as the money spent on health, dental and life insurance, which the courts ordered that he carry.

Joint Custody

He did make sure that their Christmas' were filled with presents and gifts and a tree that the three of them would pick out and decorate on the weekends prior to the holiday; however, they would get to open their presents after the holiday because they were never available, even though their orders made them available every other year.

Joint custody was the biggest joke ever played on a non-custodial father at the time because it outlined in detail all rights and actions that were to take place; however, when it did not take place as ordered, an attorney had to be hired to bring this back into the courts. Not being able to constantly afford the services of an attorney, left Roger vulnerable to anything she wanted to do. She knew this and because of it, she did anything that she wanted. He questions the court system now for its inability to enforce without cost to the non-custodial parent, orders which provide the core of the child parent relationship.

Their court orders stipulated that neither one of them could take the children across state lines overnight without notifying the other parent and providing an address and telephone number for them to be reached. To this day, Roger has never received a telephone call to inform him of any traveling plans that she had. As far as he was concerned, she never took them out of the state. However, the children were taken out of the country on vacation several times and Roger was informed after they returned. In all cases, he never even knew that she was planning a trip. On the other hand, he provided telephone numbers to her, whenever he planned to take them to his family reunion, (which only happened twice during their entire lifetime) or to his aunts house in Union Pier, Michigan. Delia would call his relatives before they arrived to question whose house this was, whether in fact they were scheduled to come and a list of other unnecessary things that was done just for the sake of humiliation.

In March of 2005, Richard who was a sophomore at Tougaloo College, was diagnosed with liver cancer. He was instructed by the college to withdraw and go home to Chicago to be with family. Roger was informed of this by his younger son Aaron. Delia has never given him any information of Richard's condition or exactly what his physical ailments are. All information that he receives comes from his youngest son. Richard was told that he might not live to see his twentieth birthday, which was May 9, 2006.

Roger have asked for prayers from colleagues and acquaintances from across the country. He has already been cheated of Richard's childhood and the prospect of being cheated out of his life entirely remains a constant dark cloud over his existence.

By the grace of God, he has survived thus far to enjoy the graduation of his younger brother. Roger loves him madly.

When Richard graduated from eighth grade to begin high school, he received a phone call thirty minutes before the graduation began. This came from his mother and she said to him, "Are you coming to Richard's graduation."

Roger said, "Of course. What day is it?"

She said, "It is today and it starts in about a half hour." This infuriated him, once again, she has engineered a method to not only keep him from this milestone, but also to give her relatives the impression, who were all there, that he did not care enough about his child to even attend his graduation. Not only was he absent from this great day in his sons life, none of his family were invited to attend. Her relatives on the other hand not only were invited but they were told in advance so that they could plan for the day.

Graduation Day

    This day of graduation for his youngest child is one of rejoicing and happiness for him because he will never have to deal with this ugly attitude ever again. The three of them; Roger, Richard, and Aaron, are taking pictures. They are laughing and joking during the graduation reception aside and away from their mother who chose to spend her time sitting with her own relatives who also does not care for Roger because of the lies that she has told them over the years. She has given her entire family the impression that he did not sufficiently support her and the children. They were led to believe that he was never available for any events that the children were involved in and that he was a deadbeat dad when, in actuality, she put every barrier possible between the children and Roger to keep him away from the events that took place during their formative years. Aaron has decided to sit with Roger's family and at this reception. On this occasion, Roger's mother , who was now eighty-seven years old and also loved her grandchildren but was also strategically eliminated from their childhood, was present. Their aunts who also had been denied visitation were also there. Aaron decided to attend college in Grand Rapids Michigan where Roger resided. He thought that the mere fact that his child would choose to attend a college in the city that he was now living spoke volumes as to the relationship that he had maintained throughout these past twenty years with his children. Aaron's mother informed him prior to graduation that if, in fact, he decided to give his father a ticket to the graduation, where the two may have had to sit in the same row, then she would not attend. She had relayed to him that the fact that he communicated with his father was a betrayal to her because it had been her over the years who had done everything for them without the benefit of Roger's presence. They now realized that their mother, who kept him away and complained to them and to her family of his absence even though he continued to attempt to be completely involved, relegated his presence.

The question today is, exactly how many men in this society have lost the most precious time of their lives? This time can never be replaced. All anyone can do at this point is think about what might have or could have been. There is no other explanation of this other than they have all been *CHEATED* of the most important time in our lives.

If she had a bill that she could not pay, she would blame their father and tell the boys that he did not care anything about them because if he did, he would make sure that all was paid up in full within her household. If a lightbulb went out in her house, she would tell them that if your father cared he would be here fixing the things that are wrong because you are his children too and he had a responsibility to take care of the dwelling where they resided. According to her, her household bills were his responsibility. She despised him because she wanted the benefit of a husband without the relationship.

The children were taught that their father did not care about them and that she had to do everything for them because she was the only one who loved them.

Parental Alienation Syndrome (PAS) is real. Parental Alienation Syndrome is referred to by the courts as "junk science" and this is not allowed in most court motions without the benefit of expert testimony when in fact it takes place everyday in this society. It does not take an expert to identify that what is being done, in cases such as this, is wrong. Parents are being alienated from their children for personal reasons by custodial parents all over the United States. For those who believe otherwise, you have closed your eyes to reality. The courts refuse to recognize PAS as a distinct possibility in relationships between non-custodial parents and custodial parents. The states of Iowa, Nevada and Maine recognize Parental Alienation Syndrome in fact these states have set aside April 25, 2007 as Parental Alienation Awareness Day. We are calling for this entire nation to set this day aside annually, following the lead of these states. If we as a society are committed to do the best thing for the child, then we must recognize both parents as an integral part of the children's lives.

I have given you all the actions and thoughts from a writer's point of view; however, what is yet to come is much more powerful than anything I might have previously said and that is the perspective of Aaron, the youngest son who lived in the house where this syndrome originated and took place throughout his life. His account will give you the feelings that he experienced and the disdain that dictated how he felt and what he did because of it. The next few chapters will begin with what will be called, *My Journey.*

My Journey

My journey began when I came to Grand Rapids to find out who my father was. I was told negative things about him, but because he was not really around to not only dispute those claims but to prove them wrong with his actions, I could not say anything differently because what she told me was all I knew. To be frank, I did not know him. In his presence, I felt like a stranger and still do.

But, in finding out the truth, I had to start by actually sitting down with my father who never got to tell me how he felt about what my mom was doing and his side of what happened. While I was talking to him, I was hit with a significant realization; I have never thrown a baseball with my father. Though most people may think that is small, I feel the small things make up the big picture, which was, he was not involved in my life to the extent that he should have.

I have had parent-teacher conferences he was never a part of, basketball games I wanted to see him there in the audience, yet he was never there and even when I had questions that were basic curiosities that surfaced as a boy that I didn't understand until I became a young adult. It saddens me to think of all the things that we missed. A scary pattern emerges from that insight. I never knew that my father was really missing from the picture. It never occurred to me that my father should be going to my basketball games. Nevertheless, the worst part about it is that my mother never told me, especially when I was younger, to invite him. Of course, because he wasn't there at the time I was growing up, I didn't think the things that I missed were significant, but when I thought about it I realized that not only did I make a lot of mistakes, but those mistakes could have been prevented if I just would have had that other parent.

Because of everything that has transpired in my life, I have the unfortunate opportunity of putting my life back together. Though my love for my mother will always remain the same, I still cannot help but to look at her with a slightly different perception. Though I control my perception of my mother, if I would not have, all these emotions and negative feelings could easily turn into hate, disgust and resentment. I just knew my mother would never do anything to intentionally hurt my brother, nor me, but in this process of denying my father access, it has done just that. I am left with scars that are difficult to heal. The worst part is that I still do not know why we were kept from my father. The way she treated him made me believe that he was a horrible person. I thought I had to protect my mother from my father. Over time this became more than just a notion. I finally said something to him in my senior year in high school.

My protective nature for my mother surfaced in late October 2005. My father called the house and we got into a big argument. At the time, we were living without heat, I was having trouble finding something to eat one night, I was going through an episode with chron's disease, and a host of other physical problems that I have inherited from my mother. There were many different things that were going wrong, my father did not know anything about it, mostly because when we were younger my mom was the one who was supposed to call him for our big events and she did not. Therefore, when my brother and I got older we were so used to not seeing him in our lives so we got accustomed to living without him.

After that argument in October, I didn't want anything to do with him, I frankly didn't care if he lived or died. Nevertheless, as the months passed, I began to think, regardless of what has happened in my life, my father should still be given a chance besides his biggest crime in my eyes was not being there. I never understood why. Whenever I would ask my mother about my dad, she wouldn't have anything positive to say and to describe him she would use every curse word she could think of. Yet the ironic thing was when I asked my dad about anything regarding my mom he wouldn't curse her name, nor would he say anything bad about her, he would tell us she was having a bad day. I never figured out why he wouldn't say anything bad about her, yet it was the exact opposite when she mentioned anything about him. I found this phenomenon interesting and it kept me curious enough to investigate the matter further.

Therefore, I decided to go to college in Michigan, even

if it was for one semester I wanted to sit down and talk with him face to face. I felt I was old enough to deal with whatever came out of my conversation with him. Before I came to Michigan, I thought it was going to be the same old thing, I thought that I would find out my father is not anything and not worth knowing and I would leave after the first semester. Yet when I actually sat down and talked to him, I began to understand how my mom used the system in order to perpetuate the negative image I have of my father. I began to understand how the judicial system supports the actions of custodial parents and how it disregards the rights of the non-custodial parent.

When I look at my own situation, I can see how my father was edged out of my life, so much that I regarded him only as a visitor. For example, if my mom didn't want my dad to see us, he wouldn't. Regardless of his efforts there was no mechanism put in place to make sure that the court orders were satisfied. When I heard my father's story, I began to understand what he went through. However, my thoughts were that my dad would come at me the same way my mother did, which was that all of his facts would be hearsay. That is what I relied on anytime my mother said anything about my father, so I thought when he would say what he had to say that it was going to be much of the same. Yet when I start talking to him, he began to pull out things that were in black and white that had been documented that represented the facts he brought to the table. This was unprecedented to me because my mother had never done anything like that, she never would talk to me about why she kept him so distant from us, nor did she provide black and white evidence of the things that she mentioned, she just mentioned that he was a horrible person.

This did not silence my curiosity nor did it conclude this chapter of my life, in fact it just left more blank pages that needed to be filled with facts. I now realize, I was and am currently left in the same position as a child that was adopted, I wanted to know my real father. In addition, when I reflect and really think about it, the system helped provide me with the drive to find out who my father is. They supported pretty much everything my mother did, if they did not, I would have had a two-parent involvement instead of one who was stretched thin.

It has me thinking even deeper, I face the real possibility of being a father one day, and just as much as this is a possibility so is the alienation of me from my children. I cannot imagine that, I would want to be the best father I could to them. I would want my children to benefit from what I have to offer them so they don't have to make the same mistakes as I did. Combining the impact that my father's alienation has had on myself and, my passion to have the capability to raise my children, I have made it my life's mission/purpose to not only be involved in my kids lives at all cost, but to make sure that no child, ever experience what I have gone through, whatever I have to do in order to eliminate complaisance of the judicial system on children that go through this daily. I am Aaron, the second of my father's two sons.

On the Inside Looking Out

Our story, my brother and I, is based on what we were told and taught about my father and our feelings of what he was about as we were on the inside of the house.

Looking out of the window, my face pressed to the glass anxiously awaiting my father's arrival. That is exactly how my brother and I felt when my mother told us "Get ready, your father's coming by." My brother and I would wait for hours until finally our mother came to the front room and told us he probably was not coming. When this pattern first started, I originally thought, well maybe he had a lot of work to do, nothing personal. Yet when it turned into a tradition that my father would not show up, I was hurt deeply. At the time, I felt like my father did not want anything to do with my brother nor me. I felt like he didn't care about what happened to us. It was disturbing to think that at such a young age, yet that was one of the deepest and longest lasting impressions that I have of my father. I was forced to live with this notion for eighteen years, before I had the ability to talk to my father about it.

I am finding out that there is an even more frightening truth about my situation, everything that I was told about my father, has turned out not to have any merit. As a child, I believed what I was told, and not necessarily, what I saw.

Many incidences in my life didn't add up, because I lived in my mothers house I only heard her perspective, therefore, I didn't know the facts about my father. For example, when my brother and I would have our noses pressed against the window, little did I know, my father did not tell my mother that he was coming and what's even more disturbing was that he didn't even know that we were expecting him. This has been an unfavorable trend in my life. I have had the unfortunate opportunity to understand some of the most impressionable circumstances in my life. I say unfortunate because I have not had the capacity to understand my mother's side of the story. I have asked her about some of my impressions that I have of my father, yet every time I bring this issue to her, I do not get an answer; she instead avoids talking about it. Therefore, I have concluded that there is no concrete reason that I should have gone through what I did. Even with that said, the courts felt obligated to support the decisions that my mom made, as opposed to assisting my father, my brother and myself to have access to each other.

After everything has been said and done, all the lying that created resentment towards my father, by my mother, has left me discouraged about my future. As a young man, I face the very real possibility of experiencing losing the ability to raise my children. I know what I have lost and I do not want my children, when the time comes, to go through the same unnecessary stress and drama that I have been.

I will begin explaining this experience by going back to one of my first memories with my father's frustrated visitation. Of course, at the time, I did not realize what was actually happening, my father's alienation from my brother and me.

At the time, my brother and I were five and six years old. My brother is a year and a half older than I am. I don't exactly remember the date and time that it happened yet I remember at what age it took place. Little did I know that this day was going to be the beginning of a lifetime of struggles, heartache and frustration.

My mother would come into our bedrooms and let us know our father was coming. "Aaron and Richard, your father is coming today," she would say before we resumed playing. Whenever my mom would tell us that my father was coming, I was automatically filled with excitement and anticipation. Usually when we went over my dad's house we would have a great time, thus we looked forward to going over to his house.

He usually would pick us up at 8:00 o'clock in the morning on Saturdays, thus we would start picking up our things in the house. One of the reasons we were so quick to pick up all the things around the house was because we were not allowed to leave unless we had picked up all of our belongings and cleaned up the house. Many times, when my father came by to pick us up, we would have already done many of the things. If not all that we were supposed to, yet regardless of what we did, frequently, we would not be allowed to leave the house to see him or she would make him wait outside until we did everything that she ordered us to do. Since we loved to go over our dad's house, we were already up early in the morning anticipating his arrival.

Some of the days that we were suppose to go over his house, we would end up staying home, upset that we didn't leave. It was not because he did not show up and left us waiting, on the contrary he would show up but because of a lack of enforcement of his parenting time, we often did not see him because she would make a momentary decision at the door after he arrived that we were not coming.

When dad arrived, he was the catalyst for any situation, not intentionally, simply because he existed and because of this, it appeared that he was at the core of many of the problems that came my way.

"Get down, hide," my mother would tell my brother and me before walking to the front door. We usually would hide in the front room, just under the window so we could not be seen but close enough so we could see things that was going on. I knew that my father was there because I heard the creak of the stairs as he ascended to the porch. "Ding Dong," the doorbell rang. My mother was pretty much already at the door waiting for him.

"I'm here to pick up the boys," my father told her.

"They are not coming," she responded.

"Yes they are, I have court orders that say that they are," he said.

"Those aren't going to do you any good, they are not coming," she said before she closed the door. I would hear these things, yet I did not really comprehend its significance at the time, but it has lasting implications on my life to this day.

In any event, after my mom would close the door in my father's face, she would tell us that he was not going to pick us up today. Immediately, I was heart broken at the news, but as children, my brother and I just went back to playing because there was really nothing either one of us could do. We would resume playing with each other for about thirty minutes before we would be interrupted with another knock on the door.

"Get down, now," my mother, said before she opened the security door. "I'm not letting them go anywhere, he called me vindictive." She was referring to a newspaper article that my dad wrote about father's rights. My mom told me that he not only wrote articles in the newspaper that were dogging her, but that he went on *The Oprah Winfrey Show* and talked about her like a dog. Trusting my mom, I believed what she told me, which is the story of my life. Years later as an adult when I asked my dad about that he pulled out the newspaper articles where he mentioned vindictive mothers. Yet when I read it, myself once again I felt like I had been mislead and betrayed, by not only my mother, but also the legal system. The funny thing is my father never mentioned my mother by name, as she said he did, nor did he call her vindictive, he was speaking generally about the population of custodial mothers that were abusing the rights of non-custodial fathers to their advantage in this article. I got a chance to see a video tape of *The Oprah Winfrey Show* that my mother referred to and again to my dismay, my father never mentioned his own personal situation. All this time, I went through life thinking that there was nothing wrong with what my mom did or said and I am now looking at concrete evidence that the things that I was taught was simply wrong and untrue. I am not saying that she should have went to jail or should have been reprimanded, not at all, but what I am saying is that it was accepted by society and enforced by the courts therefore they advocated for the alienation of my father out of my life.

When my father would return to our house with his court orders and the police, they were greeted at the door with resistance from my mother.

"Ma'am, we have orders saying that he is suppose to be here right now picking up his children, would you please let the children out," the police asked her. Depending on the situation, she may or may not comply with their request. Most of the time she would let us out after the police arrived with my dad. For those days that she wouldn't let us out of the house, we wouldn't see our father that weekend and it would be another two weeks before he had legal visitation with my brother and I. After the police would leave, she would tell us negative things about our father because of the situation that had just occurred.

"You see, your father doesn't care about you, if he did he wouldn't have tried to have me put in prison. You know that if I was put in jail, you would be put in the system," she would tell us. When I first heard that, I was scared. I thought that my father was a horrible person.

What kind of a person would try to have my mother, who I was dependent on, locked up in prison. I thought that he wanted to put my mother in prison. Immediate resentment surfaced every time I heard my mother say that. I was under the impression that my mother was the most caring person in the world, therefore if my father wanted to have her locked up; he must be a horrible person. My father would lower his head, and get into his car and drive away. I now find out that the police had no power to enforce his visitation orders. He was told that he must spend more money, get an attorney, and take her back to court for the instances that his visitation had been violated.

On top of that, I was scared of my dad as well. I thought that he was going to have my brother and I put in the adoption system. Every time he would come over to the house, I associated him with negative emotions and feelings. I now realize that from the beginning, I did not like my father.

My alienation from my father wasn't a process that was quick, it was something that happened over time and is hard to reverse. When my brother and I was younger, my dad would come by the house just to hang out with us, yet as soon as my mom would find out he was in the house, she would tell him to get out. I remember vividly many different incidences where he came over and was kicked out. He was not kicked out because he created a disturbance; he was kicked out simply because he was my father. I remember my brother and I were in our early teens, twelve and thirteen. The doorbell rang, "ding, dong."

"Who is it?" I asked my brother.

"How am I supposed to know, I didn't open the door yet," Richard replied. I heard the first security door open.

"Hey, fellas," my dad said.

"Hey, Dad," Richard said. I followed, saying the same thing when he came through the hallway door.

"What's been going on, fellas," my dad would ask before going to my brother and hugging him.

"Not too much, just chillin'," my brother told him.

"Nothing," I said to him as he approached and hugged me. As we were talking, we all moved to the dining room where the chess table was.

"Which one of you guys wants to play?" my father asked. Being the person he is, my brother immediately said, "I do."

Roger's Perspective

I must add here that I had an opportunity to come into their house, because their mother stayed on the second floor with the second floor entry door closed. My sons stayed primarily together alone without the constant supervision of their mother because she lived on the second floor of the house, which had been made into an apartment, so she didn't really know who entered or exited the house unless she came downstairs. This is neglect in its most primary form. After my children reached their teens, they had to cook and take care of their own personal needs living downstairs while their mother stayed upstairs and dictated their day-to-day lives when visiting them occasionally. Because she primarily stayed on the second floor, this would give me an opportunity to spend some time, no matter how brief, with the boys on days that I was not scheduled; however, it was brief because when their mother would realize that I was seeing the boys she immediately put me out of the house. This particular day I sat with my oldest son, Richard and, began a chess game with him. I have been a chess player since my grade school days and I am pretty good at it so it gave me pleasure to play with my sons and teach them the things that I knew. In the meantime, their mother eventually looked out of the upstairs window saw my car and came downstairs puffing a cigarette and saying, "What is this person doing in my house? Who told you two to let him in? He doesn't care anything about you." She pointed at the chandelier that hung above the dining room table, but was not on because the bulbs had blown out and she said, "If he cared anything about you that light would have a bulb in it." She gave them the impression that I was responsible for the ongoing maintenance within her house, yet I was not welcomed in the same house.

When she made her entrance and voiced her point, I would look at the boys and say, "Okay, fellas, I have to leave now," and I would hug and kiss my boys and bid their mother farewell and leave their house, still frustrated that she would never treat me like a human being.

Aaron's View

The weird thing about that is my father never argued with her, in fact, he said, "Okay, fellas, I'll see you all later," and he would leave.

It got so bad until, my mother would not even let us talk to him on the phone. "I know your father is calling on my phone," she would say to us.

I thought that maybe, he was such a horrible person that she was protecting us from him. The biggest problem with what was going on was that we were getting a lopsided perspective of who our father was. Because my mom controlled the parenting time my father had, we did not hear what he had to say, and therefore we were a product of our own environment. Dad never wasted time talking about the negative things. Instead, he referred to our time to together as Scott Men Time and we enjoyed each other and didn't focus on what he was dealing with every day of his life.

I disliked him with a passion. Every chance my mother got, she would say something else negative about him. What else was I supposed to do? I didn't realize how deeply we were impacted until years later. I realize now that I don't know my father and he doesn't know me nor my brother. It is especially bad with my brother because he is fighting for his life and is not as close to my father as I am and does not know what I know about Dad, which isn't really a lot, but my brother is struggling to survive and doesn't have the information about him that I now have nor the relationship that we are now forging.

I did not think too much of the events that took place in my life. Like any normal son, I believed my mother without question, and went along with whatever she asked. Even to this day, when we discuss matters about father's rights, oftentimes we discuss my mom, thus when we talk about the things she did, I feel emotions of resentment towards my father. He still never calls her any names he simply explains exactly what took place. I could not have been as level headed as my father is. I would probably be calling her everything that I could think of but not my dad.

Around October of 2005, I called my father, not to shoot the breeze, but to have a few words with him about my situation and our relationship as a whole. At the time I called him, we were going through some financial things at our house. We were not new to that. For the most part, when something went wrong in the house, she would say, "You see ,if your father cared about you, he would have paid our heating bill." In addition, because that was what I had been hearing for seventeen years up to that point, I did not believe differently, regardless of how conflicting the words of my mother had become with facts.

"Hey, Dad, how are you doing?" I asked, not caring about the answer.

"I'm fine and you," he replied. We went on with small talk but I was deeply concerned as how my father could simply ignore the fact that my mother was struggling financially and it did not seem to make him any difference. What I found out from this conversation was that my father was completely unaware of what was taking place in our house because my mother simply would not communicate with him. She would much rather ask one of her relatives for help than to talk to him. I do not know why she did this but it gave my mother's relatives the idea that my father was simply a deadbeat.

Roger's Perspective

Primarily, my child support was arranged by me to go through the system so that there would be a record of my payments and so that I would not have conversation about finances with their mother. At the time that we were divorced, the court gave the non-custodial parent the choice of paying the support order himself or herself or having it deducted from the paycheck by the employer. My child support was paid efficiently and kept current. Their financial struggle was based solely on their mother's inability to manage her finances. Her resentment with me was based on her idea that I had a responsibility to rescue her, in addition to my ordered child support payments, from whatever situation that she put herself in. At this point, she had opted to leave her permanent full time job and take some time off. When she couldn't find adequate employment when she reentered the workforce, she began to blame me for her financial shortfall. I however would have been willing to assist her but she never revealed her status to me and I was unaware of the fact that the heat in her house was, shut off. When Aaron telephoned me, he seemed extremely distant and I asked him what was wrong. He proceeded to tell me, "Dad, you don't care anything about us. My mother is struggling and it makes you no different."

This was a mind blower. The same house that I have not been welcomed in for years is now my responsibility, according to her, to maintain and make life comfortable for the person who has mistreated me for the past seventeen years. Yes, my children are in this house and my ex-wife had the option of sending my children to me at any time and they would have been welcomed with open arms or simply just to talk to me. Instead, she chose to indoctrinate the children with the notion that despite her choices and money mismanagement that the obligation to keep her afloat was mine solely because my children resided there. Aaron had begun to do exactly what his mother told me that he would do thirteen years ago. "I am going to make sure that they hate you," she would say to me when they were toddlers.

Aaron's actions are now resounding in great force; the realization of this sentiment was now taking shape. Aaron went on to say to me, "Dad, you don't even know me." Here is my child who I have always been there for, I have paid my child support for, I have done everything in my power to love and garner a father son relationship with who is now seventeen years old and beginning to tell me, and feel justified, the exact words that has been instilled in him from the age of three years old. Furthermore, I had absolutely no idea that my son was living in the cold. I was unaware of this because their mother would not allow me to call her house and had a major problem when she found out that my children had called me. A month passed and I had not talked to my son and I called to find out why. His mother answered and took great pleasure in telling me that Aaron did not want to be bothered with me anymore. She went on to ask, "Didn't he tell you that?" I could here the satisfaction in her voice that she had finally completely turned my child against me.

It was another two to three weeks before Aaron called me again. This time he went on to say to me, "Dad, I was thinking that despite the fact that we have disagreements, you are still my father and I should stay in contact." He continued on by saying to me," Dad, you remember you have always told me that you expect me to respect my mother regardless of what she does?"

I said, "Yes, I have always taught you and your brother that this is your mother and you must always respect her."

His next statement completely floored me he went on to say to me, "Dad, I expect you to respect her the same way."

My mouth dropped, I began to get upset and angry simply because, in my mind, this child had watched his mother disrespect me his entire life, and although I never disrespected his mother, he felt that I should be at her disposal. I went on to explain to Aaron in a calm manner that his mother commanded his respect because she gave birth to him and had kept him his entire life. His relationship and respect for his mother had absolutely nothing to do with my relationship with her.

Respect is mutual and what his mother has done to me over the years has been a blatant show of disrespect to me despite my efforts to maintain a parental relationship with the children and despite her methods of undermining this. I went on to explain to Aaron that he had no authority to expect anything from me in reference to my relationship with his mother because he had no idea of exactly what his mother has put me through. At that time, he truly did not know the extent that his mother has mistreated me over the years and it would be another year before he would actually get a chance to see and read the things that his mother has put me through.

I do not advocate for his feelings for his mother to change and I have been adamant with him about this literary effort and the consequences because I do not want to put his mother down in any way however, her actions and indoctrination is factual and he is now finding out that the things that he was taught and took for granted as a young child, although it didn't make sense, is now becoming crystal clear as an adult.

Aaron's View

All of the circumstances that surrounded this situation have to be explained separately, but they all contributed to drawing an inaccurate portrait of what my father was about. When my brother and I were younger and were still visiting our father on the weekends, we had certain restrictions about things that we couldn't bring.

My mom would get upset at us if we even tried to take a single pair of underwear. Every time we were set to go over our dad's house, we wouldn't be able to take anything with us besides the clothes on our backs. At the time, I was a confused individual. I could take clothes over my friend's house and my family's house, not my father's side, of course, yet regardless we were not allowed to bring anything to our father's house. It was so bad to where I started to wear two pairs of underwear. Even that method of transporting attire from one parent's house to another didn't work. She would check our pants to make sure that we weren't taking anything over to his house.

If she found clothes on us, we were immediately disciplined, not physically but mentally. Mentally, it took a toll over time. I began to believe that he did not deserve to have my brother and I bring clothes over to the house. However, with situations of this caliber the only people that are really being hurt is the children. Though it did not physically hurt us, we were pressured with unnecessary stress and drama, my father didn't say anything about her, but he didn't understand either why we could not bring any clothes over to his house or he often expressed his lack of comprehension with the question, why?

My mother would say to us, "What are you doing? Why are you taking clothes over your father's house?" she would say with discontent.

Of course, it was a rhetorical question; I did not know why we could not take anything over our father's house. The only reason I knew of was that she felt he did not pay any of the bills. She would then add, "Your father doesn't pay for any of your clothes why are you bringing clothes over to his house?"

I grew frustrated quickly with the situation as it became more and more apparent that the only way I could bring clothes over his house is if he paid for them while I was over there. This is significant because when he would send child support, which she never claimed was late throughout my early upbringing, she would make my brother and me open it. When she would make us open up the checks, we would be in different rooms of the house. "Aaron, Richard, come here a minute," she said. I cannot really recall the first time I was told to open a check, yet I do remember that it happened very frequently. We would walk to the front room where she was sitting on the couch. "Open that," she said to us. Since we did what we were told, my brother or I opened up the check. There was a fluctuation in the amount that was sent, but I never remember a check not being there, nor do I remember a check being under two hundred and fifty dollars. My mother would then say to us, "You see, your father doesn't care about you all, if he did he would send enough money to take care of some bills." This didn't just happen once, this happened too many times to count. Over the years, I believed that he could have sent more money to us that would cover all the bills. I was under the impression that child support was supposed to support the whole family, including the mother. With all those components combined, I was led to believe that my father did not care enough about me to help us out.

I did not realize the implications of what my mother's intentions were until I was a little older. She actually brought to my attention her thoughts about child support. "Aaron, some years from now, if you end up being divorced from your wife and have children with her, you should pay her two thousand dollars a month," she said to me. I automatically was taken by surprise as soon as she said that to me. I thought, *Two thousand dollars a month, there are some people who do not make that kind of money in a month.*

"What! Two thousand dollars a month, that doesn't make sense," I replied to her.

"You don't think that if your children were living in similar situations as you were as a child and young adult, wouldn't you want to have your children to live like that," she said.

"Of course I wouldn't want my children to have to experience any type of poverty; I would try to have custody of my children if the mother wasn't able to adequately take care of the basic needs of her household. Of course, if she had my children, I would pay child support, to support my children, but as far as my spouse is concerned, I don't think it's my obligation to pay two bills for two separate households," I told her. That's my personal feelings as a potential father one day. I would want to try to help my ex-wife as much as possible, but I wouldn't want to have to be her support system. If one parent does not have the capacity to care for a child, then I believe that child should be put with the parent that can afford their children. Yet without compromising the amount of time that they spend with that other parent.

"You are not the son I raised. I raised you to be more conscious about what you do," my mom said.

I already knew what was going to follow. She usually wouldn't talk to me if I didn't agree with what she said. I wouldn't have as much of a problem with her theory if it went both ways, but according to her, she feels that the man should automatically pay two thousand dollars a month to the mother of the children.

"Mom, I just think it's ridiculous to expect myself or any other non-custodial parent to have to pay two thousand dollars a month," I said to her.

"I don't want to talk about it anymore, you're making my head hurt," she would say before starting to make her exit from the room. This is where many issues have been created. I have come to her about problems that have developed out of parenting time frustration and just her overall attitude towards my father. Every time I would approach her with a real concern, I would be left with fewer answers than what I came with. Furthermore, to even fathom that everything that I have been through was done because of an unknown reason, is ludicrous. To me, it does not make sense, and yet, there is a trend of complaisance shown towards children in this situation, to the point where the judicial system does not even acknowledge what is actually happening.

I still do not understand, to this day, why we were supposed to open up those checks. I can speculate based off the information that I know about everything now, but at the time, I was so confused about the matter that I did not understand.

My mother even downplayed the time that I spent with my father. Whenever my brother and I would go over to my dad's house, we would have a blast. Yet, that feeling of excitement and anticipation whenever I would go to my father's house over time would be intentionally diminished. She would tell us, "Whenever you go over your father's house you always have a good time, but when you come back home, you don't have those same things. He does not care about you; if he did, he would make sure that everything in this house was paid for. He would make sure you had food in your belly and that our lights are on. See he doesn't care about you." From that statement she made, I really began to think. Well, maybe she's right; if he did love us and cared about us he would make sure we didn't go hungry. He would make sure that we always had lights in the house. What I didn't understand was that my father had sent his portion of the child support to her and she simply did not manage it properly. I also had no idea that my father did not know that we were hungry some days or that our lights were out or our gas was off. He simply did not know. I started to believe that he was good for nothing. In the words of my mother, "He's a sperm donor." Since she regarded him as such and I was under her authority all the time I began to think similarly, he was just a sperm donor. Consequently, my attitude towards my father eventually evolved into outright disgust whenever I would even think about him. I didn't want anything to do with him. At the time I was not conscious of all the elements that played a role in my development, if you would have asked me when I was younger if I hated my father or not, I would tell you no. However, as time has progressed and I became a teenager, I have realized that I didn't like my father or anything that he stood for. Therefore, I did not have too much to do with my father or my father's side of my family. I never associated with my grandmother, aunts or Uncle Louis on my dad's side because I felt that they didn't care anything about me. Not necessarily resentment at the time, but I didn't want anything to do with them because I felt they didn't want anything to do with me. I began to identify with other teens who said their fathers weren't anything. I felt the same. Yet as I am writing this, I have realized that my father never had a chance to mess up. He never was given a chance to leave us in the house unattended, to abuse us, to drop us off at a babysitter, not to say that it would happen, but he was not given the chance to mess up. At least if he did something, I would have merit when I said, my father isn't anything. However, the courts felt obligated to turn a deaf ear as my mother robbed me of my childhood, the courts felt obligated to take away a crucial part of my life. I don't ever remember throwing a baseball with him. I don't remember him ever being at my games. The expectations is that as a child, your mother or your father, whoever you are living with, will communicate the different things that go on with their children's life but those contacts weren't made, and as a result, I felt that he wasn't part of my life. By the time I got to high school, I never contacted my dad to come to my games; I never thought he was important enough to be there. It did not make me any difference.

Repairing the Broken Parts

The relationship and missed times shared will never ever be replaced. No amount of money could possibly compensate for what has been lost. We have been *CHEATED* of the most important parts of our lives and that is our own basic relationship. I have taken the position of not looking back, but looking forward. I hope that we have more life to live together, communicating with each other than we have lost in the past. Today, I still harbor no ill will and wish nothing bad for their mother. This is not to say that I am not angry, on the contrary; however, my anger is directed toward a system that allows these events to take place and I do know that anger will not solve this problem individually or nationwide. In fact, part of my daily prayer is that God will bless and keep her safe from all hurt, harm, and danger.

Conversely, my oldest son who still to this day echoes the sentiments that he believes that I could have done more for them as he grew up, is currently diagnosed with liver cancer and is in the fight of his life. I understand his point of view because he really does not know the truth, but I call him regularly to pray with him and to give him something positive to hold on to. While he personally feels that I was not the father that I should have been, I think constantly of the fact that throughout their entire lives, I have never received a birthday card from either one of them because they were taught that anything connected to me had absolutely no significance. This past Thanksgiving was the very first time that Aaron actually had Thanksgiving dinner with my family and he is now nineteen years old. I do know in my heart that Aaron understands the ramifications of the culmination of the events that have led to this juncture in his life, and because of this, he is also wary that given today's judicial system, it is a distinct possibility that this, too, could become his reality.

According to the scriptures, we are to love God with all our heart and all our soul and all of our strength and love our neighbor as we love ourselves. If we all practiced this, these events would no longer exist.

Love, much love, and even more love is the only way that the broken parts will ever be repaired.

Repairing the System

In September of 2006, Aaron and I were asked to speak at a Non-Custodial parents rally held on the steps of the capitol in Lansing, Michigan, where Aaron explained to the crowd how he has been cheated of his relationship and that he would continue to fight to disallow this from occurring with future parents. I continue to tell parents never to give up and maintain their records. Your children will appreciate knowing that you have always been there despite this cruel reality. In October, we were guests on an international radio show where the two of us told the story after which we were contacted by parents across the country and even from the UK because this is indeed an epidemic. On December 6, 2006, Aaron and I both testified before a House Committee in Lansing, Michigan, because of our support for House Bill 5267, which is a shared parenting bill. This particular bill was voted on based on party lines with absolutely no regard for the millions of parents who are hanging onto the small glimmer of hope that they may be considered as important to their children. However, these hopes are dashed based not on the best interest of the child but based on partisan lines as the bill was neither passed nor defeated because the vote ended in a tie with one representative passing.

The two of us have been asked on numerous occasions to speak to different groups of non-custodial parents and we oblige every one. The only way to repair this system is to take the profit out of child support collection by the state, and for each state to recognize that with the destruction of the American family, we must expect an eventual destruction of American civilization. Ms. Carol Rhodes explains in her book, *Friend of the Court, Enemy of the Family*, just how our bureaucratic system has put the lives of parents in the hands of caseworkers whose main objective is to raise money for the collection agencies. These same caseworkers keep score based on the total number of lives destroyed. The family is the smallest corporate unit of our society. With its elimination, we face the elimination of the larger corporate units. There are fathers today who are being denied access to their children and are being raped financially to the point that they themselves are becoming the new poverty-stricken sub culture. I am appalled that the family court system does not promote family, but is actually primary to its destruction. Why do we call it family court? When will we as Americans realize that two-parent involvement is not an award, but a God-given right? When will we realize that what is in the best interest of the child is to have two parents leading and guiding them into adulthood? When will we realize that we are driving some parents to suicide? My own career has taken a back seat to the fight that I have had over the past few years and this has ultimately become my life's work. Let us put this into perspective, fighting for the notion of spending time with my children and being recognized, as a responsible parent is what I have been driven to as a career choice? I hope every elected official in this country has an opportunity to read this effort just to give him/her or an opportunity to see what this country has become. My child, as an adult, now recognizes the events that he and his brother have missed simply because the structure of our court system totally ignores the child's right to maintain a relationship with both parents and it fails to aid in family relationship maintenance.

Aaron's Farewell

I thought that it is important to share my perspective in order to illustrate the real victims who are produced by custodial parents who feel obligated to use the system to drain the other parent out of his or her natural rights to be involved with their children. In discussing my experience with this matter, I think it is important to establish that though statistically more men go through this than women do, it is still an issue that affects both sexes. It is an issue that cuts across racial barriers, class, education; it has the capability to touch any person in society. A problem, if overlooked and not properly addressed, could lead to more unnecessary problems for society in the very near future.

I feel that father's rights, and more importantly non-custodial parents' rights, should not be overlooked. I come from a situation in which my father's rights were abused, and consequently it had an effect on how I was raised and how I perceived my father. I currently am a freshman at Aquinas College, in Grand Rapids, Michigan. I came here because I wanted to talk to my father face to face. For years, I thought that he just did not really care. I lived with my mother for my entire life up until I left Chicago to pursue my education. Because I grew up with my mother, it never seemed that important to me. I spent all of my childhood within my mother's house.

"Aaron, walk in my shoes for a second," my dad said. "Imagine, you are paying child support to your ex-wife, yet you rarely get to see your children. How would you feel?" my father asked me.

"I don't know, I would do everything I could to see my children?" I responded.

"Well, imagine that you've tried everything, but despite your best efforts you have trouble being involved with your children's day-to-day lives. It's like having a brick wall between you and your children. Even though you are paying your child support, you still don't get to see your kids. How would you feel?" he said.

I mentioned that conversation because it made me think about my future. I will someday become a father, and when that opportunity comes, I would like to have the capacity to be with my children as much as possible. I never thought for a moment that I could face the very real possibility of losing the chance to raise my children, and with the divorce rate as high as it is today, that possibility seems greater and greater.

Roger's Farewell

Aaron and I are both extremely active in our quest to implement change in the family court system where children are awarded, like prizes at the weekend fair, to one parent or the other. It is our belief that the social workers assigned to the court should begin to alter their decisions and base that what is best for children is the actual positive interaction of both responsible parents. Some, if not most of these social workers assigned to the family court system, are children themselves right out of college who don't have a clue as to what is in the best interest of the families that they routinely destroy. Children are living, breathing people who deserve to know their roots and ancestry from both sides of their family and they especially deserve to maintain a positive relationship with their parents.

Divorce is something that we should not aspire to; however, in the event of it, we have an obligation to give our children as much time as we possibly can simply because they are our children and our lives.

According to Abraham Lincoln, it is not the years in your life that count, it is the life in your years. Our children inevitably become our life. Every waking moment is dictated to what is best for our children. When a parent is cheated of this, we are taking the life out of the years of these parents who are no less responsible and love their children no less than they did when they resided within the same domicile. The challenges may differ for that other parent but the bond and the relationship must remain the same. The court system must cease from being the cause of the removal of the relationship of one parent or the other and must become an advocate to maintain the most basic relationships in this society. Exactly how much longer will the courts fail to recognize that the system has been set up to perpetuate situations similar to the one that I am now writing about? Believe me; it hurts to the very core knowing that the lives of your children have been, systematically stolen from you and you cannot change the events that you have been denied from participating in.

If you have noticed, I have made an effort not to say anything negative about my children's mother as a person because this effort is not a bashing of her ways, desires or thought patterns. This is my effort to serve as a wake up call to all of the attorneys who spend their lives driving a wedge between couples in an effort to fatten their own bank accounts while inflicting long-term damage on the lives of undeserving people. This is an effort to enlighten those judges who fail to rule based on their own lives and the long-term effects of their decisions. This is an effort to wake up the custodial parents who decide how much ransom money is sufficient before they make available the children to the non-custodial parents all over America who genuinely want to do what is right for their children. This effort is to stop the child support collection agencies, who receive federal funds for every dollar of child support it collects, from further charging the paying parent for processing, simply because he/she has paid the ordered child support.

Relationships are never measured in dollars and cents, but how much quality times it consist of.

As a denied father who never gave up the hope that my children would someday learn the truth and understand who I am and what I stand for, my sentiments to all non-custodial parents in America and abroad is never give up in your fight for your little ones. They are all you really have. What you will lose if you do not fight for your children, you will never ever get that back. I am calling for all non-custodial parent groups to mobilize and organize a march on Washington to let our lawmakers know that the practices in this country are wrong. These practices must be corrected. We will not allow this system to continue to cheat us and destroy our lives.

I have given an account of my own situation; however, there are millions of non-custodial parents all over America who have stories of their own and some with much more frightening details that have taken place than the events that I have described.

With divorce rising at an alarming rate, and the population of non-custodial parents steadily climbing, if our current legislators continue to ignore this problem, then we as a group must begin to draft and elect candidates who are sympathetic to this injustice. This population certainly has the numbers to elect any candidate that it chooses from the President of the United States all the way down to our local dogcatchers. When we recognize that, we are indeed a majority. When we stop feeling sorry for ourselves and begin to act as a united group. When we understand that together we can make this country change its behavior then those precious words of the late great Ms. Corretta Scott-King will begin to become significant to non-custodial parents everywhere because we will know without a doubt that, "this too shall pass."

As I conclude, my sentimental mentality brings me to the fact that now, just as when my sons were little boys, whenever we depart company from one another we do it the same way that we have all of their lives and that is with a kiss on the cheek and the words, "I Love You."

Printed in the United Kingdom
by Lightning Source UK Ltd.
135778UK00001B/145/A